Dedication

My two oldest granddaughters, Jessica Zottola and Amy Masoni patiently and quietly listened to my initial telling of the underwater adventures of Willie Walleye. This book is dedicated to them.

Acknowledgments

I would like to acknowledge a number of individuals who encouraged me and have been involved with the development and publication of this book. I want to thank Chris Moroni, publisher, for her continued interest and consistent advisement in the development of this book. Thanks. Illustrator, Nancy Scheibe, developed fantastic illustrations of Willie and friends. Her artistic dynamism put life into each story.

My wife Marsha and our two daughters, Sarah Masoni and Theresa Drift assisted me with finishing touches on the manuscript. Our sons, Joe, a publisher of science fiction and Josh, a father for the first time, supported our efforts in the development of this project. Lorraine Smith, a friend and co-worker at the University of Minnesota made significant contributions to my writing. In addition to suggestions for *Willie Walleye,* we wrote many scientific articles during our tenure at the U of MN.

If I have forgotten others that should be acknowledged, then chalk it up to my reduced memory capacity and accept my silent acknowledgement.

Dr. Z. aka Ed Zottola & Grandpa

Willie Walleye

UNDERWATER ADVENTURES

michele!
enJoy!
Dr Z
Ed Gottald

Dr. Z

Illustrated by **Nancy Scheibe**

Singing River Publications, Inc., Ely, Minnesota

Original illustrations by Nancy Scheibe

Published by:

 Singing River Publications, Inc., Ely MN
www.singingriver.com

Book design: Dorie McClelland, Spring Book Design
Printed in Canada by Friesens

ISBN: 978-0-9789870-6-0

Contents

The Beginning   1

Willie Finds and Rescues Wendy Walleye   13

Grandpa Walleye, the Sage of the Lake   16

An Encounter with Max Muskie   23

Wendy and Willie Go to the Prom!   27

Pictographs   36

Willie Goes Flying or Fun With an Eagle!   43

Three Sunny Pescalleros!   49

Willie Finds a Rock Band   55

Peek-A-Boo   60

Cock-a-Doodle Doo!   64

French Fries   68

Willie and Bernie Catch a Couple of Fishermen   73

Beverage Can Bonanza   79

Wilderness Area

Pictographs   Reeds

Water Lilies   Pine Island

Chicken Ran

Big Reef

Rock Band Stand

Lazy Point

Parking Lot

Boat Landing

Grandpa's Cave

N

Willie's Boat

E   W

Wild Rice Patch

S

Picnic Island

Cozy Fish Cafe

Big Fish Lake

**Approximately 15 miles
wide, 30 miles long.
(Map not drawn to scale.)**

Swimmers' Island

School Bus Parking Lot

Swimmers' Beach

The Beginning

Years ago, in a small bay on the west end of a very big lake in northern Minnesota, a fish named Willie Walleye was born. Big Fish Lake is near the Boundary Waters Canoe Area Wilderness (BWCAW). It is about 30 miles long and 15 miles wide at its widest point. It has 15 islands, many bays and sandy beaches—and one bay that is full of wild rice.

Many years ago, the Ojibwe Nation named the lake *Zaaga'gan Niibowa Giigooyug* (Lake of Many Fishes). Later, settlers took part of the Ojibwe name and called it Big Fish Lake.

Willie Walleye comes from a very large family of fish. He has hundreds of brothers and sisters. Like all fish, Willie hatched from an egg. When his mother laid her eggs, she deposited hundreds of them in a big group. Papa Walleye swam over Momma Walleye's group of eggs and fertilized them. Without Papa Walleye's fertilizing Willie's and his siblings' eggs, they would never have hatched.

Momma and Papa swam around the eggs, protecting them from other fish that might want to eat the eggs. After many days, the family of fish eggs hatched into little fish called 'fries.' The fries swam around in one big group while Momma and Papa looked very pleased.

Papa said, "Momma, we should name each one of our little fries." Momma said, "Oh Papa, what a great idea!" So they began . . . Alice, Bob, Carl, Doug, Ellen, Fred, Georgia, Howard, Isabel, Jack, Kyle, Lucy, Marilyn, Noel, Olga, Pauline, Quentin, Rose, Sylvia, Tom, Ursula, Vivian, Willie, Xerxes, Yolanda and Zack." WHEW!!!

Then, Papa Walleye said, "We will never get all of these fries named. I am done. . . ." Momma Walleye agreed. So they swam off leaving the group of fries to take care of themselves. And they did.

Swimming together in a large family school, the Walleye family of fries was able to move about and find food. One fry named Willie decided to strike off alone. Willie was different from the others. He was independent. He stayed at the head of the school so that he could benefit from the safety of its large size. Yes, Willie was special right from the beginning.

• Willie was the first one to be born.
• Willie had eyes that were much bigger and brighter than the others.
• Willie could swim faster than his brothers and sisters.
• Willie was the first walleye fry to catch and eat a worm.
• Willie had markings on his sides that were different; they looked like "Ws."
• Willie was adventuresome—always searching for new places to discover.

The small fish grew bigger and remained in a big school. Now they were called minnows. They still swam and hunted for food together.

One day as the minnows were swimming around, a big shape blocked the sunlight above them. A dark shadow covered them. The small minnows didn't know what to do! Willie looked up and was startled by what he saw. He yelled to his family," SWIM! Swim as fast as you can!! A big fish with his mouth open is blocking the sun. He looks like he wants to eat us for lunch!"

Willie swam as fast as he could. He got away from that big fish. But many of his brothers and sisters ended up as lunch for that big muskellunge. (He was a monster muskie!) Willie

looked back at him and yelled, "Some day, I will get you for eating my family for lunch!" The big muskie just swam away with a big grin on his face. Willie swam away too, but he was sad because he had lost all of his playmates.

Soon Willie noticed another big fish looking at him; he was a walleye just like Willie. The big walleye asked, "Willie, why are you so sad?" Willie responded, "A big fish just ate my family for lunch!" The older walleye replied, "That was Max the Monster Muskie. He is a mean fish who loves to scare and eat minnows. You have to watch out for him."

Willie was very angry. He shouted out, "I want to get back at him for devouring my brothers and sisters. Then he looked at the older fish and asked, "Who are you?"

"I am Grandpa Ole Walleye," the old fish responded. "You can call me Grandpa. I am the oldest walleye in the lake. I know how to survive in the waters of Big Fish Lake."

He then went on to say thoughtfully, "This is what happens in these waters. Big fish eat little fish and little fish eat smaller fish and it goes on and on. You either eat or get eaten. You have to be on the lookout for trouble all of the time. Come with me, Willie Walleye. I will help you take care of Max Muskie and any other big fish that may give you problems."

The two of them swam slowly through the lake until they came to a dark hole under a big rock in the clear green water. Grandpa told Willie, "This is where I hang out. Stay

with me for a while. I can show you how to get bigger and stronger. I can show you some of the tricks that I've learned on how to survive in this big lake."

"First you have to learn to swim fast. I want you to swim as fast as you can to the end of the cave. Then, turn around and come back."

Grandpa thought for a moment and then said, "When I yell "GO," swim as fast as you can! Are you ready?" All of a sudden, Grandpa yelled "GO" in his loudest fish voice.

Willie swam as fast as he could but he couldn't see in the darkness of the cave. He kept hitting his head on the sides of the rocks. Finally, with a little struggle, he reached the end of the cave. He took a deep breath. In the darkness, he turned and started back. Willie saw Grandpa waiting for him in the dark murky water. "You were too slow. You must go faster." Grandpa mustered another loud fish voice and again yelled "GO!"

Willie turned and went again. This time he didn't bump into the rock walls as before. Grandpa told him, "Not bad for your second try. That was much better." With a con-cerned look on his walleye face, Grandpa said, "We will continue this training every day until you can swim faster than Max Muskie! Now, let's rest and find something to eat. We can work on your swimming again tomorrow."

After many days of training and eating with Grandpa Walleye, Willie grew bigger and faster than the other wall-eyes his age in the lake. Grandpa told him, "There is noth-ing more that I can teach you now. You have become faster, smarter and stronger than I. You are on your own now. You must go away and begin your life."

Willie was sad. He had grown to care for Grandpa Walleye. It was lonesome swimming around Big Fish Lake by himself. Willie needed a friend. One day as Willie was swimming and eating, he happened upon another lonesome fish. He was a bit different. His markings were different. He had black stripes along his sides and a red eye.

Willie got up his courage and asked the new fish, "Who are you?"

The new fish answered in a sad fish voice, "My name is Bernie Bass and I am lost. I cannot find my school."

Willie said, "My name is Willie and I am a walleye." Willie continued, "Walleyes and bass are not usually friends. Grandpa told me that bass and walleye don't get along well." Bernie looked sad as Willie continued. "We could be related. Maybe you could be my cousin!" He went on, "I lost my family too."

At the same time, Willie and Bernie both said, "Why don't we hang out together?" "Okay!" said Willie. "Okay!" said Bernie. Even though they were different, they quickly became good pals.

The new friendship began immediately. Willie and Bernie began to swim around the lake. Willie showed Bernie his special hiding places. Bernie showed Willie his special hiding places. Together they found a new and interesting spot on the west side of the lake where they could watch humans at work and at play. The two fish buddies spent a lot of time there. One morning as they were watching human children play, they noticed that they had lined up next to an open area that was covered with a dark material. Soon a large yellow vehicle arrived and the children started to get into it.

"What are they doing? Where are they going?" asked Bernie.

"I don't know," answered Willie.

   While they were watching, Grandpa showed up and
watched the children get into the large yellow vehicle.
Grandpa knew a lot about humans.

   Willie asked Grandpa, "What are they doing? What are
those big letters on the side of the vehicle?"

   Grandpa replied, "Those letters spell SCHOOL BUS!
It takes children to school." Willie and Bernie looked at

each other with wonder in their eyes. Then Bernie asked Grandpa, "Why don't we go to school on a school bus?"

With a fish twinkle in his eye, Grandpa laughed and said, *"Because fish are already in schools!"*

Willie and Bernie looked at each other and smiled. With the grin still on his face, Willie said, "My Grandpa Walleye sure is smart!" And they all swam off to find a bite to eat.

Willie Finds and Rescues Wendy Walleye

Willie was cruising Big Fish Lake one morning looking for something to do. He swam into a dense growth of water lilies when he heard strange noises. It sounded like 'help' in walleye language. Willie continued to swim through the lily pads until he found the source of the noise.

He found a walleye barely able to move, all wrapped up in fish line. The fish was a female walleye and she was struggling mightily to get untangled. Willie swam over to her and looked her in the eye. "Could you use some help?" he asked.

"Of course I need help!!" she sputtered. "Why do you think I am yelling for help?!"

Sheepishly Willie replied, "Okay."

He swam around her trying to figure out what to do. Then he spotted the end of the fish line hanging below her. "What would happen if I pulled on the end of the line?" he wondered. He took the end of the line in his mouth and pulled it tight as he swam away. It worked! The line came off rapidly. In the process, the girl walleye spun around and around.

"Wow! What a trip!" she exclaimed. She tried to swim away but continued to swim in circles because she was so dizzy.

Watching her, Willie chuckled (just a little) and then asked her, "Do you need more assistance?"

"No," she said, "I like swimming in circles."

"Okay," said Willie, trying to be polite. He started to swim away.

"The she yelled, "Of course I need help, you silly fish. Please get over here and help me get straightened out!"

Willie chuckled quietly again as he swam over to help

her. He pushed her back and forth until she stopped swimming in circles and began to swim in a straight line. She
responded by thanking him and giving him a kiss on the
cheek. Willie was very surprised. "Wow! He said to himself.
"That was interesting. (He said this because he had never
been kissed before.)

"Can you do that again?" he asked. She responded by
kissing him again—this time on the lips. A real fish kiss!

This female fish impressed Willie. "What's your name?"
he inquired.

She responded in a quiet voice, "Wendy."

"I like that name. It goes with my name which is Willie,"
he said.

Then Willie decided to ask her another question. He
asked, "How about we hang out together?"

Wendy was quiet as they swam along. Willie noticed
several leeches swimming near by. He quickly swam over to
them, grabbed a few in his mouth and swam back to Wendy.

"How about a snack," he asked her.

In response, she opened her mouth and took the leeches
from him.

"Thank you," she said. After swallowing, she spoke again.

"I'd like to hang out with you, but I want to be able to do
my thing without having you around all of the time."

"Sounds good to me," Willie concurred.

Then the two of them began to explore the lake together.
Their friendship grew better each day.

*"Isn't it great how wonderful things happen when you help
one another get out of trouble?"* Willie smiled at Wendy.
They would spend many more days together.

Grandpa Walleye, the Sage of the Lake

One day, Willie was visiting with Grandpa Walleye. He liked to visit because Grandpa had lots of good stories to tell.

Willie asked him, "Grandpa, how come you have not been caught by fishermen when so many other walleyes have been caught?"

"Well, Willie," Grandpa began. "I learned a trick a long time ago. I learned how to take the bait off a fisherman's hook without getting caught on it."

Willie asked, "What is the trick, Grandpa? I would like to learn it so that I can fool the fishermen too!"

Grandpa replied, "My family started out as a big school just like yours did, Willie. I watched most of my brothers and sisters get caught by fishermen. As I watched, I noticed that the bait was always stuck onto a metal hook. Sometimes it was very loose on the hook. Sometimes it wasn't. They look like this." Grandpa drew pictures of the hooks and bait on a big rock. He used a small sharp rock as a pencil.

"I also noticed that when the others were caught, it was usually because they opened their mouths wide and sucked the bait into their mouths as fast as they could. When this happened, the hook caught them in the mouth and away they went into the fisherman's boat. So I practiced using an old rusty hook with some line on it. I found them on a rocky ledge near a shallow weed bed. First, I hung the line and hook from one of the reeds and learned that if I slowly bit the bait rather than sucking it in, I could remove the bait without getting hooked. Then, I practiced and practiced until I was confident that I could do it without getting caught."

"One afternoon, I went out, found a boat full of fishermen and tried my trick. It worked!! I ate at least a dozen worms that day without getting a scratch! It still works today. Why, just yesterday I had lunch from two fishermen who were using shiner minnows for bait. Those shiners were delicious.

"Would you like to learn how to do this?" Grandpa asked Willie.

"You betcha!" Willie shouted back.

Grandpa told Willie that he had not taught any other walleyes his secret method and warned him to share it only with good friends who would not teach these tricks to other kinds of fish. Willie raised his right fin and promised, "I swear that I will not teach this trick to any other fish."

Then they swam to Grandpa's secret training place. Willie saw all kinds of fishing rigs hanging in this small underwater cave.

"Wow Grandpa!" said Willie. "Where did you get all these rigs?"

"That's another trick I will show you," said Grandpa.

Grandpa continued with Willie's lesson. "You grab the fishing line above the hook. Then, quickly hook it onto a log or beneath a rock on the bottom of the lake." Grandpa grabbed one of the lines and showed Willie what to do. Then he said, "The fishermen will try to pull the rig off the bottom. Eventually the line will break. Then you can unhook it and take the trophy hook back home."

Willie liked what he heard and asked Grandpa to continue. Grandpa said, "You can try this after you learn the bait trick. The bait trick works only when they are fishing with live bait. It will not work when the fishermen use fake plastic baits."

As he spoke to Willie, Grandpa looked at him to make sure that he was listening and understood what he was being told.

Under the watchful eye of Grandpa Walleye, Willie learned how to trick the fishermen and take their bait. He practiced and practiced until Grandpa said, "Okay Willie, now you can go and try it out on real fishermen."

Willie and Grandpa swam around for a while until they found a big pontoon boat with several fishermen aboard. The men were having a good time catching lots of fish. Grandpa said, "This is a good fishing boat to finish your lessons and to get a free meal as well!"

Willie watched the fishermen for a while and finally decided to give his new-learned skill a try. He saw a hook with an earthworm attached and headed directly for it. Slowly he sucked the worm into his mouth and bit it off before his fish lips reached the hook. After that, the line was reeled up, new bait was attached, and the same hook was dropped into the water again. Willie sucked up the worm again. The fishermen kept feeding him until Willie

had taken at least a dozen worms from the same hook. He had a great time!

Then, he and Grandpa Walleye "high-finned." Grandpa had taught Willie to "high-fin" some time ago. It is a trick that the fish do when they're having fun or celebrating a victory.

Giving a "high-fin" is equivalent to humans giving a "high-five." To do a "high-fin," the two fish swim toward each other. When noses touch, they swing into a vertical position and slap their tails together with a loud "WOP!" Then they swim away.

Willie thanked Grandpa for teaching him new tricks. Willie told Grandpa Walleye, "Sometimes it is fun to get an easy meal. This is one I had to work hard to get. *That's okay, because hard work never hurt anybody!*"

Then Willie asked Grandpa, "Is it okay with you if I teach my pal Bernie Bass the bait-stealing tricks?"

He replied, "Yes. But you cannot tell anyone else. If all the fish knew how to do this, the fishermen would get smart and figure out other ways to catch us." Willie raised his fin and promised, "Bernie Bass will be the only one."

With that, Grandpa and Willie turned themselves vertically and slapped their tails together. Then they shouted in unison, "That's 'high-finning!'"

An Encounter with Max Muskie

Willie and Bernie were hanging around the reed patch in one of the small bays of Big Fish Lake. They were looking for something good to eat. As they swam around they noticed an old wooden boat sunken in the deeper part of the bay. They swam down to the lake bottom to take a good look at it. "Cool," said Willie. "We can use this as a place to hang out."

Bernie was swimming around and investigating the inside of the hull. With a smile on his face he said, "I agree. It looks like we could hide in it."

They swam back to the reed patch and continued to look for food. There were a few bugs hanging on the reeds. Willie and Bernie found them and enjoyed their snack.

"Not much here," Willie noted. "Let's go down to the bottom and see if we can find a few crawdads or leeches." So they started down to the bottom of the bay.

Suddenly, there was a dark shape above them! They looked up and saw Monster Max. He seemed to be looking for something to eat. Willie whispered to Bernie, "We better get out of here or we will end up being lunch for Max Muskie!"

As they started to swim away, the big muskie saw them and roared, "THERE'S MY LUNCH!" Then he started after them.

Bernie yelled to Willie, "Swim! Swim as fast as you can! We have to get away from this monster!" And that is what they did. They swam as fast as they could, but the big fish was catching up to them. For a muskie, he could swim fast but not as fast as Willie and Bernie.

Willie yelled to Bernie, "Swim to the wooden boat! We can hide in it."

"Okay," Bernie yelled back. "Let's do it!" They headed to the sunken wooden boat. They reached the boat a few fin-strokes ahead of their nemesis.

Max Muskie yelled at them, "I've got you now!" He opened his big tooth-filled mouth to catch them.

Willie smiled and told Bernie, "Quick! Let's go through that hole in the side of the boat. He is too big to get through it."

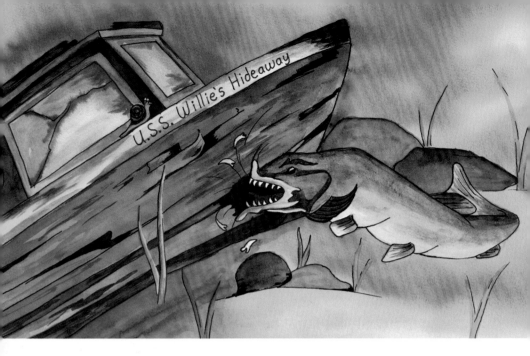

They quickly swam through that hole in the side of the boat. Monster Max saw where they went. He was swimming so fast that he couldn't stop. He crashed into the side of the boat WHAM! BAM! BANG! UGH! and knocked himself out! Slowly he dropped to the bottom of the lake beside the sunken hull and lay there—out cold!!

Willie and Bernie looked out through the hole in the side of the boat and saw Max Muskie lying on the bottom. They started to laugh and then shouted together, "We got you monster breath!" You'd better watch out for us next time or we'll do something worse to you!" Of course Max was out cold and could not hear them.

"I'll bet that he will have a huge headache when he wakes up from his sleep," Bernie said to Willie.

"Yes," Willie replied. *"Notice what we can do when we use our heads to outsmart a bigger fish rather than trying to physically out-do him."*

With enough excitement for one day, the two fish pals swam off into the waters of Big Fish Lake.

Wendy and Willie Go to the Prom!

There is a special place in Big Fish Lake that Willie and Wendy like to visit. In this spot, there is a big fancy restaurant where many humans go for entertainment. If the sun is setting and sky is clear, the walleyes are able to watch what the humans are doing.

One fine evening just before the sun was setting, Willie and Wendy stopped by to see what the humans were doing. They were very surprised when they saw many big automobiles parked near the restaurant. They watched as the people got out of their cars and walked to the restaurant.

The men were all dressed up in fancy black outfits. The women wore long sparkling dresses of many different colors. As Willie and Wendy watched this parade of fancy-dressed humans, they wondered what was happening.

Willie said to Wendy, "Let's get closer so that we might be able to hear the people talking." They swam under the small bridge that led from the parking lot to the restaurant, remained quiet under the bridge and listened.

They heard the young men telling their young lady friends how pretty they looked in their fancy dresses. The young ladies were telling the young men how handsome they looked in their fancy tuxedos. Eventually they heard several of the humans mention that they were looking forward to their evening at the Prom!

Wendy asked Willie, "What's a Prom?"

Willie did not answer her question because he did not know the answer. Instead he said, "Let's ask Victoria. She has seen a lot and knows all about what humans do." As they swam away, Willie explained to Wendy who Victoria was. "Victoria is the oldest living female fish in Big Fish Lake; we call her Queen of the Lake.

They swam around looking for Victoria and found her at her favorite spot in the lily pads, taking a nap. Willie and Wendy were not surprised to find her sleeping. Old walleyes are like older humans. They take a lot of naps. They waited until she woke up because they knew that if they woke her up she would be grumpy. If that happened, she would speak in a crabby tone of voice to them—or worse—not even answer their questions.

After a while, Victoria awoke and shook herself. She grabbed a leech that was swimming by and smacked her lips as the tasty snack disappeared down her gullet. Then she noticed Willie and Wendy and gruffly asked, "What do you two want?"

Wendy described what they had seen. Victoria listened with interest. The old queen thought for a while and finally explained, "A Prom is a special night for young humans. They get all dressed up in fancy clothes. The young ladies wear formal dresses and the young men wear tuxedos. They

eat in fancy restaurants and then go to a big ballroom where they listen to music, dance and have a good time. This may go on all night; the humans won't get much sleep."

Willie and Wendy thanked Victoria for her help and swam off. Wendy was thinking very hard. Finally she said to Willie, "Let's have a Prom!"

Willie responded, "I will talk to the guys and you talk to the girls. Then we'll see who is interested."

Willie went back to the school of fish and gathered all the male fish that he could find. He told them about the Prom

idea. Not one of them was interested. Their two main objections were first, that fish can't dance and second, that they didn't have a band that could play music. Willie swam off to tell Wendy what the guys had said.

Wendy found her girl friends and told them all about the prom idea. They thought it fantastic and immediately started to figure out how to make their fancy dresses. They were all talking at once.

"We can use the cloth in that old dress that sank to the bottom the other day."

"The claws from a crayfish could be used to cut the cloth to make the dresses."

"There are some shiny lures that have been caught on deadheads in the lake. We can use those as decorations!"

"This will be fun!"

Wendy was a bit anxious about how they were going to sew the dresses together. Just as she was getting worried, one of her friends swam up with a whole bunch of fish lines

and a couple of small hooks that could be used as sewing needles. They were all set to sew!

Wendy set up a production line. There were cutters with crawfish claws who were cutting out dresses. There were sewers with fish line and hooks sewing the dresses. Decorations were added by another group of artistic walleyes. Each dress was different. Wendy made sure that each girl had a dress that fit perfectly.

About this time, Willies swam up to report the male walleyes' decision not to participate. Before he even spoke

with Wendy, he saw the girls making the dresses. So he decided to go back to the guys and convince them that they should participate in the prom if they wanted to have girl friends. After some discussion, all of the male fish agreed to participate, but insisted that they would not wear tuxedos.

The guys asked, "What about music for the prom?" Bernie said, "We can get the Three Sunny Pescalleros to play for us at the Sandy Bar where they give their concerts.

"All right!" yelled the guys. "Let's do it!" The quickly swam to find and tell the girls.

When they found the girls, a big surprise was waiting for them. The girls were wearing gowns for the prom. Each guy swam over to one of the gals to escort her to the prom area which was a beautiful underwater cavern with filtered sunlight coming through the rocky shale overhead.

But. . . .

The girl fishes couldn't swim in their fancy dresses! They all began to scream and yell at Willie and Wendy because they couldn't swim. Willie looked at them and said, *"Of course you can't swim! You are wearing dresses, not swimming suits!"*

The fellows took their dates by the fin and led them gently through the water to the Sandy Bar, where they listened to music, danced and ate worms, grubs and leaches long into the night.

Pictographs

The north shore of Big Fish Lake is a wilderness area where no humans live. On this shore there is a very high cliff that drops straight down into the water. Centuries ago, the Native Americans that lived in this area painted 'pictographs' on tall rock cliffs. The pictures showed people in canoes, human handprints, thunderbirds, caribou, and the horizon marked by sun and water.

When the lake level was high, some of the pictographs were under water. In one of her travels around the lake, Wendy had found the pictures and was fascinated by them. She really liked to look at them. When she told Willie about them, he was not interested.

But Wendy and her friends, Wilma and Winston, would swim over to the cliffs, look at the pictographs and talk about what they might mean. One

day when they were looking at these pictures, they noticed a strange animal on the shore. It was not very big but it looked mean. It had black fur, a long tail, bright shiny eyes and paws with sharp claws. They did not know what it was.

Wilma swam over to the spot where this strange animal was drinking water and asked, "What is your name and what are you?" This animal raised its head and looked around. It did not know where this question had come from. Finally it noticed Wilma and responded, "My name is Midnight and I am a cat. I like to eat fish."

She asked him, "Why do you have such a funny name, Midnight?"

"I am so black in both color and character that you and your friends better get away from me before I catch you all and eat you for lunch!" Wilma laughed at him because she knew that the water was too deep for this cat to catch her.

She returned to her two friends and told them about Midnight, the mean cat that eats fish. They looked frightened and said, "Let's get out of here."

Wilma said, "No. Let's have some fun with this mean cat. If we go over to the shore near the big drop-off, the cat cannot walk out to catch us. Grandpa Walleye told me about wild cats. They don't like water and they are very poor swimmers. We could tease him. He can't catch us in the water."

Okay," they said. "Let's do it."

The three of them swam over to the shore, stuck their heads out of the water, and squirted water on Midnight. He yelled at them, "I am going to catch you and eat you!"

The three walleyes yelled back, "You can't catch us. Try it and see what happens."

Midnight sat by the water and thought about it for a few minutes. He concluded that if he got those fish riled, they would come closer to shore and he could catch them. He yelled back, "I am going to catch you and feed you to my cat pack. What do you think of that?"

The three walleyes squirted him again and laughed at him. If you have ever heard a fish laugh, you would know that it is an unbearable sound and hurts the ears of cats.

The more the fish laughed at him, the angrier Midnight got. Finally he could take it no longer. He jumped into the water, thinking it was shallow enough to walk out and grab the walleyes. Guess what? He ended up over his head, under water!

Midnight was scared and quickly swam back to shore. *Do you know what stroke cats use when they swim? They dog-paddle!*

Midnight scrambled up the shoreline as fast as he could. He stopped for a moment and yelled back, "I am going to catch you all very soon!"

Wilma, Wendy and Winston laughed so hard their stomachs hurt. They had tricked the cat that likes to eat fish! Then, still giggling at the fun time they had with Midnight, they turned and headed toward the big bay they called home.

Willie Goes Flying or Fun With an Eagle!

Willie and Wendy were looking for juicy mayflies but were not having much luck. Grandpa Walleye had told them that this was mayfly season. Mayflies are insects that hatch in the late spring or early summer, usually May and June. They live for one day only. They hatch from eggs and larvae on the bottom of the lake, swim to the surface and fly around to mate. They fly up and down and around and around look- ing for a mate. When they have found their mate, they drop back onto the surface of the water to deposit their eggs. Sometimes, they simply drop from exhaustion or dizziness (from flying around in circles). Because they are many in number, they make good fish food.

Willie told Wendy, "I am going to get closer to the surface of the water to see if I can spot mayflies up in the air. When he got there, he was so busy looking for flies, he did not see the eagle flying around. Suddenly the eagle dropped down, skimmed the water and grabbed Willie with his claws. Willie was small so the claws did not puncture him but surrounded him and kept him in the grip of the eagle.

Willie thought: *This doesn't look good! Look how far out of the water I am. We are really flying high!*

"Why am I not enjoying this?" he said to the eagle. The eagle told him to be quiet. *Ha!* Willie thought. *He doesn't like his victims to talk to him. So if I talk, maybe I can get out of this mess.*

Grandpa Walleye had taught Willie: "When in trouble,

begin a rambling conversation." So, Willie started off by say-
ing, "Hi, Mr. Eagle. My name is Willie. What is yours?"

The eagle responded with a bit of frustration in his voice.
"My name is Ernie Eagle. Now be quiet. I am taking you to
my nest You are lunch for my eaglets."

Willie continued nervously. "Well Ernie, I was going to
have mayflies for lunch but now it looks like I'm going to *be*
somebody's lunch."

Angrily, Ernie said, "Be quiet!"

"Ernie," Willie continued, "how many children do you
have? Are you married? What's your wife's name? Does she
like fish for lunch? What are your children's names? Do you
have more than one eaglet? What do they look like? Are
they as beautiful as you? Can they fly? Do you stay here all

Then he stretched out his tail until it reached the Ernie's belly and tickled it. Soon the majestic eagle started to giggle. Willie tickled him faster and pretty soon Ernie was laughing so hard that he dropped Willie back into the lake.

As Willie made a big splash, Wendy was right there waiting for him. He told her all about his big ride in the beautiful blue sky with Ernie Eagle.

"Well, Willie," said Wendy, "it just shows you that if you work hard at it, you can get out of trouble without using violence."

Three Sunny Pescalleros!

In a rather large "pad" of water lilies lived the Three Sunny Pescalleros, three musical sunfish named Sam, Sunny and Sunny-Side-Up! The third fish was called Sunny-Side-Up because he liked to swim upside down! They were mischievous—always looking for trouble and finding it!

Next to the lily pads was a public swimming beach with a sandy swimming area. It was the favorite swimming hole of the local children. Sam, Sunny and Sunny-Side-Up loved to go to this swimming beach and watch the humans swim. Their favorite trick was to swim quickly up to the ankles of the swimmers and give them a quick bite on the ankle or toes. Their nip did not break the skin but the startled the swimmers. They would jump up and down in the water yelling that a 'something' had bitten them. The three Sunny Pescalleros would laugh and laugh at their own joke. Sometimes the children would run from the water and not return for quite some time.

One day when the three were having fun chasing the humans from the swimming beach, the

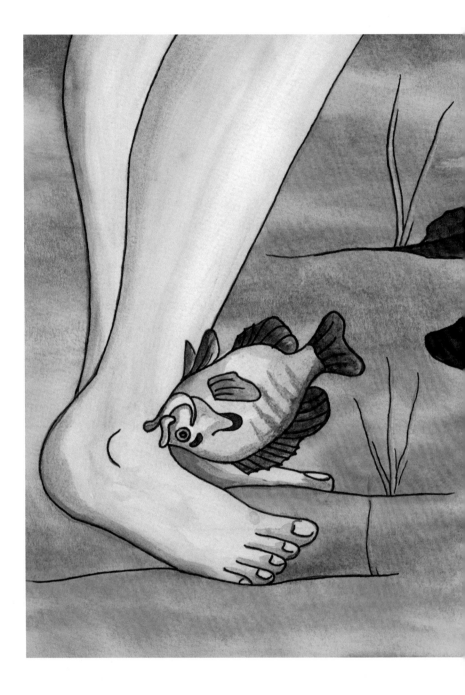

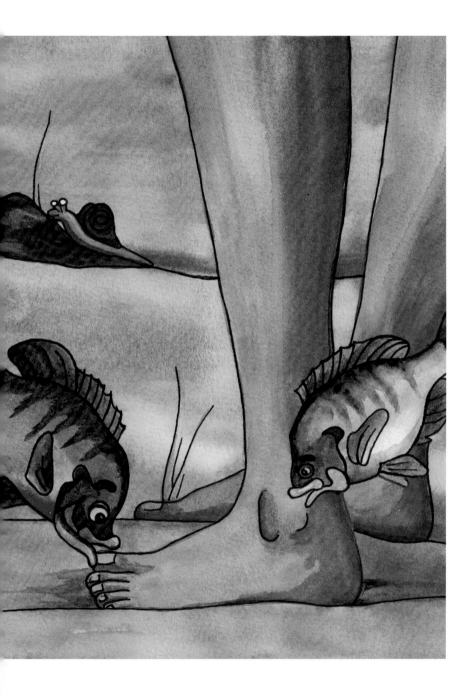

water became very dark. Something was hiding the sun! The Pescalleros looked at each other and wondered what had happened. Sunny-Side-Up, who was swimming upside down, looked at the surface of the water and saw the reason for the darkness: Max Muskie was watching them! He was drooling and licking his chops!! He was picking out his lunch!!!

Sunny-Side-Up looked at his buddies and yelled, "SWIM! Swim for your lives!" The Pescalleros darted away from the muskie, swimming as fast as they could swim. Max Muskie charged after them.

"What shall we do?" cried Sunny, his voice full of fear.

Suddenly, Sam had a lifesaving idea. "Look over there!" Sam yelled. "There is a small hole between those two big rocks. If we swim as fast as we can and dive through that small opening, we will escape Monster Max!"

Max Muskie was hungry and that made him careless. He was so intent on catching his lunch that he did not pay attention to where they were going. Just as Sam's tail disappeared into the small hideout in the rock, WHAM! BAM! SCHAZAM! Max Muskie hit the rock going full speed ahead. He expected a fish dinner but knocked himself out instead!!

"What happened?" Max asked himself as he drifted slowly to the bottom of the lake. Then he shook his head a couple of times and checked his teeth to make sure that they were all there. His head ached as he began to swim away—very slowly. This was the last time he would try to make a meal of those Pescalleros.

Behind the rocks that hid them, the three sunfish were laughing and high-finning and slapping each other on the back. "We did it!" they chorused. "We fooled that ugly mean fish and escaped!

"It just goes to show you," said Sunny. "Even when playing, one has to look out for trouble!"

Willie Finds a Rock Band

Willie and Bernie had just finished a lunch of crawdads and sat lazily in the sun. Bernie Bass said, "Let's go over to Lazy Point and gobble a couple of worms for dessert."

So they did. Lazy Point is named because it is a place where fishermen sit in their easy chairs and dangle worms into the water, hoping to catch a fish. Mostly, the fishermen fall asleep. That makes it easy for Willie and Bernie to grab worms off hooks. (Grandpa Walleye had taught them well!) But after a couple of tasty snacks, the two friends decided to look for a more interesting activity than eating.

"What are we going to do now, Bernie?" asked Willie.

"Well," said Bernie, "Wendy told me that there was going to be a big party over near the beach."

So they swam toward the beach. As they got closer, they heard unusual noises. They could see all kinds of fish swinging and swaying to the rhythm of a sensational musical cadence. There wasn't much melody but the beat was fantastic. It sounded like rocks hitting together creating an impelling rhythm. Out of curiosity, Willie asked one of the dancing fish swingers, "What's going on?"

"We now have a rock band of our own!" one of the dancing fish joyfully responded. "They are called The Three Sunny Pescalleros!"

Willie and Bernie looked around and found three sunfish beating the rocks together with fantastic energy. They recognized them immediately—Sam, Sunny and Sunny-Side-Up—the three that like to tease human swimmers.

This rock band had collected all kinds of rocks—big rocks, little rocks, flat rocks, round rocks, and broken rocks of granite, shale, hematite and quartz. Each type of rock added to the quality of their rock band sound. They played a variety of tunes, some good and some not so good. Some tunes had a poor sense of beat because their sound waves were dis-

torted in an underwater current. However, sometimes this current was good when the band used electric guitars.

It was fun to be there. Everyone was having a great time swinging, swaying, jumping, high-finning, twirling and dancing to this rhythmic beat.

Suddenly, everything came to a screeching halt. The water in the area of the beach had become very dark. Willie and Bernie looked up. Max Muskie was heading for the party. He had dinner on his mind—again!

Willie yelled, "Everybody swim for your lives! Here comes Monster Max!"

The party broke up. Fish scattered in every direction. The Three Sunny Pescalleros looked at their rocks, looked at Max

Muskie and began to throw rocks at him using their tails as catapults. Willie and Bernie did the same. But they could see that this was not going to stop the big muskie.

Willie shouted to Bernie, "Over here!! Help me with this long stick!"

They each took one end of the stick in their mouths and swam toward Max. The big fish was intent on catching as many fish as possible. His mouth was wide open. Bernie and Willie jammed that stick past those sharp teeth into the muskie's open mouth! Max Muskie could not close his mouth! It was stuck open. He didn't know what to do. He

just swam around with his mouth open trying to figure out how to remove that stick. Finally he swam away, looking for anyone who would help him. As he swam away, he thought: *Some day I am going to get those two fish! They will not even know what hit them!*

The Three Pescalleros gathered their rocks and began to play their musical rhythms again. The fish all returned and gave Willie and Bernie high-fins for their brave deed!

Sam said to Willie and Bernie, "Thanks for saving us from that big mean fish. You two are heroes! The party continued far into the evening.

Peek-A-Boo

The Three Sunny Pescalleros were enjoying their day, doing dorsal fin-springs, flipping out of the water and nose-diving back into the cool depths of the lake. Off in the distance they saw Harry Northern Pike lazily swimming toward them. Sonny said to the other two, "Let's have some fun with Harry."

Now, Harry Northern Pike was not as swift as Max Muskie. As a result, he was easier to trick. The sunfish thought for a few minutes. Sunny-Side-Up said, "Remember those rocks that we found just west of here?"

There were three big boulders at the deep end of a large reef. Each boulder had a little cave where one small fish could hide. "Let's go over there and play 'peek-a-boo' with old Harry."

"Okay," nodded the other two in agreement.

Off they went, making sure that Harry saw them swim past. He immediately followed them. The Pescalleros reached the safety of these special rocks and hid in the crevices. Harry swam over to the rocks but could not find them anywhere. Back and forth along the reef he swam, looking for them, but he just couldn't see them.

Suddenly Sam swam out of his hole and yelled loudly at Harry, "PEEK-A-BOO!"

Harry swam towards Sam with his mouth open, expecting a delicious sunfish snack. Sam darted back into his hiding place. At the same time, Sunny swam out of his cave and yelled, "PEEK-A-BOO!"

Startled, Harry turned toward the noise. His forward momentum drove him ahead. WHAM! BAM! He collided with Sam's boulder. His mouth was open and he lost a couple of teeth. Shaking his head to clear his thoughts, he spotted Sunny-Side-Up hollering, "PEEK-A-BOO!" and aimed his eyes and mouth in his direction. Sunny-Side-Up waited until the last possible minute and then dived back into his hiding hole.

Guess what happened? Harry knocked out more teeth. He *still* couldn't find a sunfish for lunch. "Where were those tasty sunfish hiding?"

Meanwhile, Sam was having a good laugh at Harry's expense. Harry heard Sam laugh and headed toward Sam's cozy corner, swimming faster than ever. Sam yelled, "PEEK-A-BOO!" and disappeared. Sunny did the same. So did Sunny Side Up! Harry was now swimming in circles, bumping into the reef boulders and losing lots of teeth. His mouth was beginning to hurt.

"How could one sunfish be in so many places? Harry was very confused. His jaw hurt. His brain was dizzy from swimming in circles. He was not thinking clearly. He was also not paying attention to where he was swimming. WHAM! BAM! Again he hit the rock with his mouth open and lost the rest of his teeth. A toothless fish cannot eat another fish, even if he could catch one!

The three Pescalleros scooted out of their rock caves and shouted, "PEEK-A-BOO, Harry! We tricked you! You had better see a dentist!"

Don't worry about Harry losing his teeth. Northern Pike easily grow more teeth. Harry knew that he would grow new teeth quickly.

Sam turned to his friends and said, *"See what we can do when we work together?"*

They continued to laugh and then swam away doing high-fins.

Cock-a-Doodle Doo!

It was a cool summer evening. Bernie and Willie were swimming close to shore looking for food. They were very near the farm of Stan Olson as it fronted the lake. Suddenly they heard a strange sound. "Cock-a-doodle do!" It was repeated several times, "Cock-a-doodle do! Cock-a-doodle do! Cock-a-doodle do! Willie heard it repeated so many times that he figured he could make that sound. Immediately, he tried to do it. "Cock-a-doodle do!"

Bernie told Willie, "It sounds almost the same. Why don't you do it so that other animals can hear it?"

Willie stuck his head out of the water and yelled, "Cock-a-doodle do" several times. You might think it strange that

a fish could do this, but remember, Willie is not an ordinary fish. He is very talented and can mimic the sounds of many different animals.

The two fish friends waited to see if Willie's crowing

would get a response. Suddenly they heard, "Cock-a-doodle do! Who are you?"

"We are Willie and Bernie, a couple of vagabond fish," Willie responded. "Cock-a-doodle do! Who are you?"

It took a while for a response. Then they heard, "I am Roger Rooster. I am boss of the yard and I am boss of the chicken coop."

"What's a chicken coop?" Willie yelled back.

"A coop is where chickens live. Where do you live?" responded Roger Rooster.

"We are fish and we live in the lake," said Bernie. "Where else do you think fish live?"

"Don't get smart with me," said Rodger. I am boss of this chicken yard."

"Sure," said Willie. "You are a card!"

"You make us laugh!" piped Bernie.

That kind of talk made Roger Rooster sulky. He yelled back, "I am boss of this yard and I won't take back-talk from you, whoever you are!"

Willie and Bernie were having so much fun that they started to laugh. Have you ever heard a fish laugh? It is a funny sound, like bubbles popping rapidly as they rise to the surface of the lake. The sound can be heard for miles around.

The laughter of the fish hurt Roger's ears. He was getting angry as he trotted down to the lake's edge. He crowed, "I am Roger Rooster, the boss of the yard and of the beach here in front of this chicken coop."

Willie yelled, "The beach is ours. Try and take it away from us!"

Roger ran down to the lakeshore. He was very upset.

Willie and Bernie squirted him with water again and again. Roger was now furious! He started to run into the water to chase those two fish that were teasing him. Suddenly, he found himself up to his neck in water and remembered that he couldn't swim! He began to splash around and gasp for air as his head went under the water several times.

Willie and Bernie saw what was happening. They did not know that a rooster could not swim. Quickly they swam over to help Roger push his head out of the water and put his feet on the beach. Roger stumbled out of the water and stood on the beach. One wet chicken!!

As he tried to shake water off his feathers, Willie and Bernie watched and then asked him if he was OK. Roger replied, "I am just a bit wet but I will dry soon."

"We are sorry we teased you. We were having fun at your expense," Willie told Roger. "We won't do it again. Let's be friends, not enemies."

"Okay," said Roger Rooster.

They all agreed that next time they would simply exchange "Cock-a-doodle dos."

As they swam away, Willie said to Bernie, "We learned a lesson. It's not nice to tease someone you don't know. If you make them sad or angry and they won't be your friend. There will be no more teasing of other animals by us. Agreed?"

"Good thoughts, Willie," said Bernie. "No more teasing animals."

Willie replied with a big, "YOU BETCHA!"

67

French Fries

Bernie Bass and Willie were on the look-out. Something didn't smell very good. They were swimming near their favorite human-watching place. It smelled like garbage.

"Let's go over to the bridge. Perhaps the smell is coming from the humans' picnic area," said Bernie.

When they arrived, they noticed that there were several small boxes on the bottom of the lake. Some boxes were white, some were red and some were decorated with stripes. There were also some long brown skinny things drifting along with the current. They looked like worms but they were not alive.

Willie sniffed one and said to Bernie, "They don't smell like worms. I am going to take a bite." "Ugh!" he said as he spit it out, "It's terrible—soft and mushy with no flavor. Salty. Hmmmm."

He tried another. So did Bernie. Yuk! No good! They wondered what these things were.

"Maybe these things came in those boxes. Let's go and look at them."

So they did. They swam to the bottom of the lake and found several boxes stuck in the sandy bottom. They could not read the printing on the boxes so they swam back to the bridge to find out where these boxes were coming from.

Standing on the bridge were some human teenagers. They were eating these long wormy-looking things from the boxes. Then they spotted Bernie and Willie.

"Let's see if these fish will eat French fries!" They began to throw French fries into the water. Willie and Bernie watched as more French fries sank to the bottom of the lake.

"They are polluting Big Fish Lake," cried Willie. "There must be something we can do to stop this!"

Bernie and Willie thought for a while. "I have it!" exclaimed Willie. "We will throw this garbage back. The humans will have to get rid of this food some other way."

"How are we going to do that?" Bernie asked.

"We will use our high-fin technique to do it," replied Willie. "One of us will grab the French fry in our mouth and flip it upward. The other will do a high-fin, hit the French fry and send it flying out of the water. It is kind of like what we did when we catapulted rocks at Max Muskie."

"Okay," said Bernie. "But first let's practice. We have to send these things quite a distance."

So they practiced. Bernie would grab a French fry in his mouth and

flip it up with a quick turn of his head. Willie would then bat it with his tail and away it would go. After a few misses and several more attempts, they got the procedure down pat and could flip French fries out of the water. Then they went back to the bridge.

The young humans were still at the bridge looking for fish. When they spotted Bernie and Willie they began to throw French fries at them.

"NOW!" commanded Willie as the French fries landed in the water.

So they started high-finning French fries back at the humans. French fries were flying out of the water! In fact, several hit the lake-polluting humans. Willie and Bernie flipped them back just as fast as the humans threw them into the lake. The teenagers couldn't figure out how the fries were coming back at them. Finally they ran out of French fries and, in disgust, threw the boxes into the lake.

Willie grabbed one of the boxes and called out to Bernie, "Let's send these back also." And so they did. The young humans didn't know what was happening. They ran to their parents and cried, "The fish are throwing things at us!"

The parents laughed and said, "Fish can't throw things back at you. Go and play somewhere else and stop bothering the fish."

Willie and Bernie were laughing and high-finning.

"Let's hope that this will teach them not to throw trash into our lake. We fish have to show these folks that *our lake is not a garbage dump.*"

Then they swam off to tell Grandpa Walleye what they had done.

Willie and Bernie Catch
a Couple of Fishermen

As usual, Willie and Bernie were cruising around the lake. They visited all of their special spots but nothing interesting turned up.

"Let's go over to the big reef to see if we can find some yummy leeches for lunch," said Bernie. So they did.

By the time they got to the big reef, it was late in the afternoon. There was a fishing boat parked directly over the reef. A couple of fishermen were standing up in the boat, fishing. A number of empty drink cans were slowly sinking to the bottom of the reef. Fishing lines were hanging limply over the side of the boat. There was almost no bait on the hooks. These fishermen were more interested in what they were eating and drinking than in baiting hooks and fishing.

Now earlier in the summer, Willie had taught Bernie Grandpa Walleye's trick of stealing bait from a hook. Willie said to Bernie,

Willie said to Bernie, "Let's jerk their lines a couple of times so that they think they are getting a bite."

They each grabbed a line above the hook and gave it a strong jerk; the fishing poles almost fell out of the boat. Quickly the fishermen

73

grabbed their rods and reeled in their lines. The bait on their hooks was gone!

Then they began to complain about 'missing a big fish.' Willie and Bernie were laughing under the boat. They could hear the fishermen talking about putting big night crawlers on their hooks.

Willie and Bernie gave a big high-fin and said, "Yeah, we are going to get a good meal after all." They watched the baited hooks drop to the bottom of the lake and followed them down.

When the hooks were on the bottom, the two friends quietly and quickly nibbled the night crawlers off the hooks, as Grandpa had instructed. After swallowing the last bite, they swam above the hook, caught the lines in their mouths and gave the lines a big jerk.

The fishermen saw their poles bend 'big' again, quickly ran to them and reeled in their lines. But there were no fish on the hooks. In disgust, one man said to the other, "We are almost out of big night crawler bait. How about putting just half a worm on each hook? Then when the fish go after the bait, we've got them!"

Again, Willie and Bernie were listening to this conversation. They were hiding under the boat.

"Let's really trick them this time," said Willie. "Let's not wait until the hooks hit bottom. Let's grab them as they are sinking, hook the two lines together under the boat, give the lines a big jerk and see what happens."

The two fish carefully retrieved the lines as the hooks were sinking, keeping the lines loose so that the fisher-

men would not feel the lines move. Slowly they brought the hooks together and connected them. The hooks were barely covered with bait so it was easy to connect them to each other. Then, with the lines in their mouths, they jerked them very hard. Their strong tails helped them jerk and swim away from the boat with the line in their mouths.

The fishing poles bent double! The men saw this, grabbed their poles and shouted, "We must really have a big one this time!"

They reeled in their lines, the poles almost breaking. Harder and harder they pulled but did not realize that they were hooked together, battling each other!

They continued to go back and forth almost falling out of

the boat. Both of them were getting upset and tired of this battle with the unknown fish. Simultaneously, they both pulled very hard on their poles. They pulled so hard that they both stumbled and fell out of the boat!

Willie and Bernie watched the fishermen splashing around in the water, trying to get back into their boat.

"Looks like we caught ourselves a couple of fishermen," said Willie looking at Bernie.

They swam away stopping every few minutes to have a laugh and slap fins in a high-fin salute celebration.

Bernie remarked, *"For once, the fish caught the men!"*

Beverage Can Bonanza

The summer day was so clear that the sun shone deep into the waters of Big Fish Lake. Willie, Wendy, and Bernie decided to check out the swimming beach. There was usually some entertaining human activity for these three good friends to observe. As they swam toward the beach, Wendy noticed that the sun was glinting off something at the bottom of the lake.

"What are all those shiny things at the bottom of the lake?" asked Wendy. Both fish replied at the same time, "I don't know."

Willie swam down to the bottom and came back to the others with a report. "They look like beverage cans to me. You know—they are the containers from which humans drink liquids."

"Sure is a mess down on the bottom of Big Fish Lake," commented Bernie.

Suddenly, as they were resting, there was a noise on the surface. In that very spot, a beverage can plopped into the water. They looked up and watched it fill with water and sink slowly to the bottom. Then there was another plop—and another! More cans were "raining" down on them.

"Look at the mess! Nothing good will come from cans at the bottom of the lake. We have got to stop the humans from throwing cans into the lake and polluting our home," a very frustrated Wendy thought out loud.

"Let me think about it," said Willie. And he did think—hard! Finally Willie turned to Bernie and asked, "Do you think we could do the same tail flip with these cans as we did with the French fries?

"Let's try it and see," replied Bernie.

Willie continued, "We will not be able to pick up the cans on the bottom. They are filled with water and are too heavy. We will have to try the tail flips with the new beverage cans as they land in the water—before they fill with lake water. If we hit them with our tails as they enter the water, we should be able to toss them back on the beach. Let's try it now!"

Willie explained the execution of the tail flip to Wendy.

She understood and actually could do it better than either Willie or Bernie. She was small and fast.

"As soon as you see a can land in the water, flip it back," Willie told the other two.

"Let's spread out so we don't hit each other with our tails or the flying cans," suggested Wendy.

So they spread out and waited for a can. Within minutes a can landed next to Willie. He flexed his tail and sent it sailing back to the beach. Wendy was the next one to get a can and Bernie got one soon after as well. They were getting accurate at flipping the cans back to the humans.

On the beach, the humans couldn't figure out why all the cans were flying around. They were constantly calling to one another, "Look out! Here comes another one!"

They would pick up the can and throw it back into the lake. But then, the humans soon grew tired of throwing cans back and forth. Finally they left the area to go and play volleyball. When the beach was empty of humans, the fish were happy.

I hope that they have better aim with the volleyball than they did with the cans," commented Bernie. "Now, let's see what we can do about the cans under water that are too heavy to flip."

Willie had been thinking about this problem. After a short time he said, "I have an idea. Why don't we find some carp? They are bottom feeders. They have mouths that are under their chins. Maybe they can push the cans off the bottom and onto the beach."

"Great idea, Willie!" exclaimed Wendy. "Let's go to look for them."

"This way," said Bernie. "I think they may be over at Garbage Bay. There is a lot of food on the floor of that bay."

They all swam over to Garbage Bay and sure enough,

there were a bunch of carp rooting around at the bottom
of the bay. Willie swam around until he found Mario Carp,
the head of the Carpolia Gang. He explained the situation
to Mario to determine if they might be interested in helping
clean up the swimming beaches.

Mario asked Willie, "Why don't the humans clean up
after themselves? They are the ones that made the mess!"

"Many humans do not like to clean up the messes they
make. Also, the beverage cans have sunk to the bottom of
the lake and the humans can't see them," responded Willie.

Mario was thinking about whether or not to accept this
clean-up project. Willie decided to make an offer to the
Carpolia Gang that might appeal to them. He said to Mario,
" If you help us move the cans off the lake bottom up to the
beach, we will let you and your gang root out other edible
material from the bottom of the lake in that area."

Mario said that he would
have to talk with the gang to
determine whether or not they
wanted the work. So he rounded
them up and they had a discussion about this project.

Finally Mario came back to
Willie and said, "We will do the
work but we also want any food
that might be found in the cans."

"Great!" said Willie. He called to the Carpolia Gang, "Follow me to the swimming beach!" They all followed and arrived at the beach in record time.

"Here we are," said Bernie. "Please get started on the cans."

The gang began to root and roll cans right up to the water's edge where they deposited them in small piles. Willie went looking for some muskrats to help move the cans further up the beach. He found Mark Muskrat, the big boss of the muskrats in Big Fish Lake and explained what he wanted the muskrats to do.

"No sweat," Mark replied. "Sounds like fun for us. We can roll them up the beach into a large pile for the humans to collect and recycle."

They all got busy and cooperated, each one doing what he was good at doing. When the sun rose the next morning, the beach was covered with piles of rusting beverage cans that had been place there by the labor of the Carpolia Gang and the muskrats under the supervision of Willie Walleye and Bernie Bass.

Willie, Bernie, Wendy, Mario Carp and Mark Muskrat looked at the beach with all the rescued cans. The lake bottom was clean! What fun it was to organize this work project with the help of so many others. They thanked the Carpolia gang and the muskrats for their help.

'We did a good deed." Bernie said to Willie.

"Thank you for organizing the work party," Mario and Mark said together. "And thank you for asking us to help clean up Big Fish Lake. They went on, "It would be nice if the humans would clean up their own messes."

Wendy, Willie and Bernie were very happy to hear their new friends' excitement.

"We agree with you, but humans don't see the bottom of the lake. We do. Maybe we have to be organized to keep our lake clean."

"Let's organize a group to do beach and bottom clean-up." Willie was so happy he said, "We could call them the Fish Scouts." "This could be done on a regular schedule," Willie thought.

"Good idea!" he said. Let's start working on a plan."

Happily the group listed their accomplishments.

"We were able to get help from other fish and animals that don't normally work together. We cleaned up the swimming beach for the humans. We showed them how much mess they have made on the floor of the lake. We showed them how to clean it up."

Willie was ready for a nap. The hero of Big Fish Lake swam away planning his next adventure.

Dr. Z is Ed Zottola,

a retired professor of food microbiology from the University of Minnesota. He caught his first fish at the age of six using a safety pin, a piece of string and a worm. It was a small trout, not a keeper. From that time on, he was "hooked" on fishing.

The Willie Walleye stories were originally bedtime stories for his two oldest grand daughters. After a couple dozen of these fish tales were well received by the children, he wrote them down to share with others.

Ed is still an avid fisherman. He has fished the streams and lakes of Minnesota and Oregon. Other fishing adventures include the Pacific Ocean off the coast of Oregon, the Inland Passage to Alaska, the streams of Alaska and the salmon streams of Nova Scotia. Currently he is out fishing somewhere in the region of northern Minnesota, still wondering what walleyes do in their spare time.